Secret, Secret

D1120255

First published in 2016
by Jessica Kingsley Publishers
73 Collier Street
London N1 9BE, UK
and
400 Market Street, Suite 400
Philadelphia, PA 19106, USA

www.jkp.com

Text and illustrations copyright © Daisy Law 2016

All rights reserved. No part of this publication may be reproduced in any material form (including photocopying or storing it in any medium by electronic means and whether or not transiently or incidentally to some other use of this publication) without the written permission of the copyright owner except in accordance with the provisions of the Copyright, Designs and Patents Act 1988 or under the terms of a licence issued by the Copyright Licensing Agency Ltd, Saffron House, 6–10 Kirby Street, London EC1N 8TS. Applications for the copyright owner's written permission to reproduce any part of this publication should be addressed to the publisher.

Warning: The doing of an unauthorised act in relation to a copyright work may result in both a civil claim for damages and criminal prosecution.

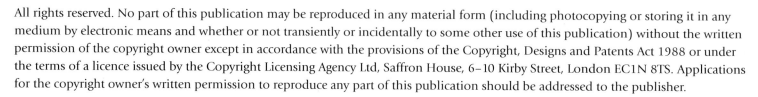

Library of Congress Cataloging in Publication Data
A CIP catalog record for this book is available from the Library of Congress

British Library Cataloguing in Publication Data
A CIP catalogue record for this book is available from the British Library

ISBN 978 1 78592 042 4
eISBN 978 1 78450 294 2

Printed and bound in China

Secret, Secret

DAISY LAW

Jessica Kingsley *Publishers*
London and Philadelphia

Secret, secret.

Keep or tell?

or SHOUT and YELL?

A sad secret.

A man
on the moon,
loony-tune,
mad secret.

A heart secret.

A head secret.

A dust bunnies
under the
bouncy
bed secret.

A little secret.

An ENORMOUS secret.

A BIG, HUGE, ROARING,

"Do you think they saw us?" secret.

A new secret.

An old secret.

A makes your insides scared and stone-cold secret.

Your secret.

My secret.

A cross our hearts
and hope to die secret.

A quiet secret.

A LOUD secret.

A sky-high, floaty clouds, *PROUD* secret.

A dark secret,
a bright secret.

A crisp skies,
starry-eyed
night secret.

Keep
or
tell?

Stay hush-hush
or SHOUT and YELL?

If
someone
told
you...

...what
would
you
do?

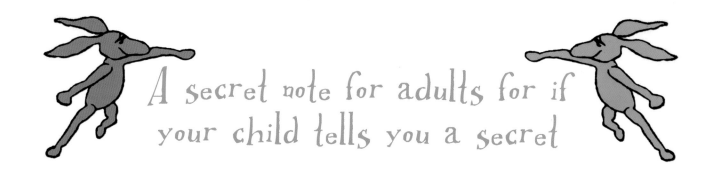

A secret note for adults for if your child tells you a secret

Keeping any kind of secret can cause a child to be anxious. If, after reading this book, a child speaks to you about a secret they are keeping it is important to respond sensitively.

Even keeping a secret about some positive news or a surprise party can cause a child to become stressed – the very notion of keeping something hidden can upset or unnerve, and cause them to experience feelings of guilt, worry and a sense of responsibility beyond their years.

If a child speaks to you about having to keep even the most innocent secret, put yourself in their position and respond with compassion and understanding. If a child trusts you enough to reveal a secret, they deserve their faith in you to be respected and supported. How you respond can affect whether a child is likely to place such faith again in future.

It's common for children to experience feelings of guilt or shame about personal issues, such as bedwetting, and to be anxious for their secret to be kept private. A child who reveals a personal problem is putting a lot of trust in whoever they disclose to, so a sensitive response is key. If a child talks about another adult asking them to keep something like bedwetting a secret, it may mean the child feels they are to blame in some way, and reassurance that the fault does not lie with them is needed.

Likewise, any response to a 'confession', perhaps about a lost or broken object, should first be supportive rather than critical. What might seem insignificant to an adult can be deeply troubling to a child's sense of conscience.

Secrets kept between friends can also carry a lot of weight and anxiety for children. Children can feel they are 'telling tales' if they reveal such a secret, and there may be peer pressure or even a threat of punishment if the secret is revealed.

Such pressure can be even more pronounced if telling a secret involves a family member, and the act of telling could get them into trouble. The sense of double standards and confusion over a loved one behaving in a way that the child understands to be wrong can be deeply troubling, and they will need reassuring that sometimes even really nice people can make mistakes – remind them that their first loyalty has to be to themselves and their own wellbeing.

If a child tells you about a problem with bullying, bear in mind they may have experienced threats and coercion and be fearful about the consequences of telling. Children can be subjected to bullying for a long time before they have the courage to speak up, and some only do so when they are at breaking point.

For disclosures of bullying, neglect or any form of abuse, it is important to listen sensitively and take swift action by contacting an appropriate agency.

Revealing serious abuse is a huge step for a child. They don't know it, but their future emotional health is dependent upon being allowed to express the complex range of feelings which the abuse and the abuser have caused them to feel. So, the way you react to a child's disclosure of abuse can have a profound effect on how they feel about themselves and their experiences. Children pick up on reactions and may close down if they think you're reacting negatively.

If a child discloses abuse, take the SAFE REPORT approach:

S   Support and reassure

A   Actively listen and be calm

F   Fact gathering – go slowly

E   Explain the next steps

REPORT and note down the disclosure immediately.

Survivors of abuse can go on to lead happy, healthy, productive lives, just like anybody else. The key is accessing the right kind of help – on the next page is a list of links to information you need to access if a child has disclosed abuse. Following disclosure, many people can feel further abused by individuals or systems treating them inappropriately or insensitively, so letting a disclosing child know that it is safe to report it to you is the first step.

A SAFE REPORT should lead to the right kinds of changes taking place for the child: intervention and healing.

Contacts for further information

UK

Young Minds
www.youngminds.org.uk
The voice for young people's mental health and wellbeing.

NHS
www.nhs.uk
Professional viewpoints from health specialists within the
National Health Service.

Childline
www.childline.org.uk
A children's charity set up to respond to crisis points of abuse
and mistreatment from the child's perspective.

NSPCC
www.nspcc.org.uk
Addressing all forms of child abuse through practical
interventions.

USA

Prevent Child Abuse America
www.preventchildabuse.org
Campaigning for great childhoods nationally.

Darkness to Light
www.d2l.org
A national organisation aimed at ending child abuse in the US.

Childhelp.org
www.childhelp.org
Linked to the national child abuse helpline for the whole US.

Parentmap
www.parentmap.com
One of many regional parenting groups throughout the US.

Australia

Raising Children
www.raisingchildren.net.au
The Australian parenting website.

Australian Childhood Foundation
www.childhood.org.au
Prioritising safety and recovery from abuse.

Kids Helpline
www.kidshelpline.com.au
Advice for kids, teens and parents.

Childwise
www.childwise.org.au
National helpline and counselling for preventing, recognising
and responding to child abuse.